THE YOUNG FRONTIERSMAN Series - Book 2

ALLEGIANCE

A Story of the Ohio Country

I0546024

Matthew Blaine

MILFORD HOUSE

an imprint of Sunbury Press, Inc.
Mechanicsburg, PA USA

MILFORD HOUSE

an imprint of Sunbury Press, Inc.
Mechanicsburg, PA USA

For information about special discounts for bulk purchases, please contact Sunbury Press Orders Dept. at (855) 338-8359 or orders@sunburypress.com.

To request one of our authors for speaking engagements or book signings, please contact Sunbury Press Publicity Dept. at publicity@sunburypress.com.

FIRST MILFORD HOUSE PRESS EDITION: March 2024

Set in Adobe Garamond Pro | Interior design by Crystal Devine | Cover by Lawrence Knorr | Edited by Lawrence Knorr.

Publisher's Cataloging-in-Publication Data
Names: Blaine, Matthew, author.
Title: Allegiance : a story of the Ohio country / Matthew Blaine.
Description: First trade paperback edition. | Mechanicsburg, PA : Milford House Press, 2024.
Summary: Young Barnabas Locke enters the Ohio Country as a trader of goods but on a secret mission. He is captured by the renegade Simon Girty, runs a gauntlet, is ambushed, rescues his Abenaki friend, and battles an avowed enemy. Resourceful, he cleverly disentangles himself from intrigue, arrest, and revenge to arrive safely at the Mississippi River.
Identifiers: ISBN : 979-8-88819-188-0 (paperback).
Subjects: YOUNG ADULT FICTION / Action & Adventure / General | YOUNG ADULT FICTION / Historical / United States / Colonial & Revolutionary Periods | FICTION / Historical / Colonial America & Revolution.

Designed in the USA
0 1 1 2 3 5 8 13 21 34 55

For the Love of Books!

In memory of
Dan Shechtman,
teacher, historian, knowledgeable trader
in period knives, and good friend.

CONTENTS

ACKNOWLEDGMENTS

Every storyteller needs trusted first readers to offer edits, suggestions, and criticisms that combined make the story being told smarter, sharper and more engaging. By good luck, the following volunteered their time and keen eyes to the task.

Jim Glenn
Denise Glenn
Stephen Balchunas
Alane Balchunas
Jerry Treon
Dan Shechtman

INTRODUCTION

THE CHARACTER OF Barnabas Locke introduced me to historical figures of his era. In researching this sequel to *Fidelity*, I discovered the real-life Simon Girty, a native son of Colonial-period Harrisburg, Pennsylvania. Girty was a pivotal figure during the Revolutionary War and long afterward in the Ohio Country beyond the Allegheny Mountains. He and his family were captured by Lenape Indians, who murdered his stepfather and dispersed his mother and the four brothers to various tribes. Simon, at age 15, was given to the great warrior Guyasuta, Chief of the Ohio Senecas, and lived for seven years under his tutelage near Lake Erie. Simon Girty loved both his white family and his Seneca family. He turned his back on the American cause during the Revolutionary War but never on humanity, as he was alleged to have done. He illustrates the complexity of the individual caught up between two cultures in this rapidly shifting human tide of peoples from the East westward into the Ohio Country. Other historic characters, such as John Harris II and

Alexander McKee, appear in this book among the many fictional ones.

An inexpressible debt of gratitude is owed to Dr. Lyman C. Draper, the indefatigable mid-19th century collector of the lives and exploits of those frontiersmen who left their marks on the Ohio and Kentucky Countries. Dr. Draper devoted decades of labor to extensive research, ferreting out manuscripts, memoirs, newspaper articles, letters, and public and private records. He traveled thousands of miles to interview hundreds of witnesses and contemporaries who lived well into the 19th century and from second and third-hand accounts by their descendants. He almost singlehandedly rescued these notable figures, such as Simon Girty and his great friend and foe Simon Kenton, Daniel Boone, George Rogers Clark and innumerable others, from the exaggerations, misconceptions, and fabrications often more popular than the unvarnished truth.

I give thanks and credit to Phillip W. Hoffman, author of the enlightening biography *Simon Girty: Turncoat Hero*, published in 2008. This biography inspired me to weave Simon Girty into my fictional narrative, which is true to the spirit of that time without necessarily being true to actual events. I regret any failures in historical accuracy.

As a disclaimer, I identify myself as a "storyteller," not as an expert or historian in any field.

Be assured I have done due diligence in consulting authentic sources for information and inspiration.

Matthew Blaine
Storyteller
July 2022

ONE

———— + ————

ENCOUNTERS

At the ferry crossing, Barnabas Locke, astride his sturdy gelding, Little Bay, looked west over the broad waters of the Susquehanna. The river was running fast from heavy, late-spring thunderstorms but was not carrying much debris. The water was too high for horse and rider to ford, much less with pack horses in tow. In midstream, standing at the bow and stern of the ferry barge, three men with long poles strained against the current as they returned to the eastern shore. Here was Barnabas's starting point for the long trek west into Indian country.

As he watched the polers bend to their work, a young voice accosted him. "My grandpa would not allow to have those horses eat the leaves off his mulberry tree." Startled, Barnabas noticed the barefoot youngster pointing to the two horses he had tied to a low limb of the mulberry. The taller vigorously rubbed his shaggy neck against the trunk while the smaller munched new leaves.

"Who is your grandpa, lad?" he asked.

"Read his name for yourself," the boy replied impertinently and pointed again.

Barnabas dismounted, giving the reins to the boy to hold, and examined the handsome upright marker, a tall block of carved limestone half-buried in the uncut grass. "John Harris," he read with interest and below the name, "The Friend of William Penn." His year of death was 1748.

"Say, laddie, was it your grandpa who was tied to this tree and nearly burned by Indians?"

Happy for a fresh audience, the boy regaled him with the tale already passing into legend. Barnabas was more interested in locating a livery stable for his mount and pack horses and lodging for himself. He had already traveled a long way from the Green Mountains of Vermont to arrive at Harris's Ferry.

Young Robert Harris offered to show him the way. "Hop up," Barnabas said to the boy, still holding the reins of Little Bay. On foot, he took the lead strap of the taller pack horse while the smaller, with a mouthful of mulberry leaves, fell in behind. Their destination was Harris's Tavern and Livery Stable.

At the tavern, he engaged the proprietor, the son of the John Harris buried above the river, in conversation about the route westward to Fort

Pitt. Mr. Harris obligingly offered to sketch the milestones of the route for Barnabas, who presented the first blank page of his ledger to him for that purpose. Barnabas and his horses would cross the Susquehanna here at Harris's Ferry, take up the Simpson Ferry Road into Carlisle, and there connect with Forbes Road on its direct path to Fort Pitt at the Forks of the Ohio two hundred miles west.

"It's the Ohio River that marks the border between Kentucky—Virginia claims that wilderness as its western county—and the Ohio Country to the north of the river. That land is claimed by a whole bunch of Indian tribes. The Forbes Road is not a rough road but hard traveled by all sorts. Not all of them honest or without evil intent. We are at war, young man. Best to keep your eyes peeled." He handed the ledger back to Barnabas. "Now, might I ask, Mr. Locke, what line of trade are you in?"

"My father traded with Indians along the Canadian border. He taught me to bargain smart and honest, and his Indian partners taught me their speech and ways. Right now, I've got two pack horses in your paddock that I'm looking to load with trade goods suitable for settlers and Indians alike. Cloth of all kinds, blankets, thread and needles, steel awls, axe-heads, folding knives, ribbons, beads, kettles, tinware, fish hooks." Here,

Barnabas paused to take a breath. "The usual goods that everyone needs but no weapons or hard liquor. I don't aim to incite more violence than we already got. War is bad for business."

Mr. Harris chuckled. "Funny you should say that, Mr. Locke, in just those words. A trading partner of mine in that country, Monsieur Bellevue, says exactly the same in his correspondence."

Barnabas hid a startled reaction to that name. With a seemingly casual interest, he asked, "Would you recommend Monsieur Bellevue as a middleman between me and your trading enterprise? As I am coming new into this territory, I am needful of establishing my credit amongst the traders."

He spared a rare smile for Mr. Harris and pulled from his coat pocket a sealed letter on stiff paper. "Here is my letter of introduction, Sir. The name may be known to you—Deputy Quartermaster General Udney Hay, under whom I served in the Saratoga campaign."

Mr. Harris considered the serious young man before him. New blood to supply his chain of outposts was welcome. A strong, smart, young man, already seasoned in the protocols of the trade and who had served in the war, could be an asset. The name of Quartermaster Hay was, in fact, well-known to him. He took the letter and scanned it quickly, noting the date of 20 March 1781 and the Quartermaster's high praise for Corporal Locke's honesty, diligence and bravery in the performance of his duties. With confirmation of his first good impression of the young man, he said, "Let us talk over a meal about how we may best serve our mutual interests." Later, when they rose full from a hearty dinner, the two men shook hands to seal their agreement.

Some days later, having passed through Carlisle, Barnabas encamped for the night in a secluded grassy swale well off Forbes Road. The smoke of his fire rose discreetly in a thin, straight column. The three horses, his riding horse and the two pack horses were hobbled and cropping grass. He had removed all tack and packs, whisked sweat and dirt from the horses's coats and picked their hooves clean. They had each received a feedbag of corn from the rations they carried.

Barnabas reclined amidst a pile of trade goods covered with an oiled tarp. In his hands, he held his German-made pistol, emptying it of powder and ball, swabbing the barrel and lock clean, and rubbing a bit of bear fat soaked into a rag over the gun for its protection. The pistol had been a gift, and he kept it clean and close. Aside from his tomahawk, this pistol was his sole weapon. During his militia service as a courier, he had not carried a long gun. They were heavy, cumbersome, and often snagged by overhanging branches. His job had not been to fight but to carry information. Besides, in his new capacity as a trader of goods, he wished to present a peaceable presence, welcome at any settlement, post or campfire.

Laying the reloaded pistol aside, he prodded the fire. From his pocket, he pulled the letter of introduction, which had earned him the confidence of Mr. Harris. If found by parties opposed to the American cause with that recognizable signature, it could be a liability. He held the stiff paper by a corner over the flames and watched the firm black letters curl into ash. This letter had been replaced in his pocket with a letter of credit, establishing his bona fides as a legitimate trader of goods and signed by John Harris. In pencil, lists of goods to be sold and their values now covered several pages of his ledger book, following his first notations as to the price paid for his two pack horses and their rigging.

Listening to the hobbled horses graze, he was reminded that the pack horses, though scruffy and nondescript, still required the dignity of names. Both were sorrels without white markings of any kind, shaggy and plain-faced. Indeed, the taller of the two had a distinctly Roman nose. They had proven to be sturdy and sound, amiable towards one another, and no nuisance to either Little Bay or to himself. And yet, beside the quick, sleek and responsive Little Bay, the two seemed without character. Barnabas sighed, postponed the naming yet again, and dowsed the fire.

Nodding off, he felt the prickling sensation of being watched. Alert, one hand on his pistol and the other grasping his tomahawk, he rose and brought the horses closer into camp. He sat, counting stars, but no one approached, and he heard nothing untoward. Too tired to keep his eyes open, he slid into his bedroll and into sleep with the pistol still in his hand.

At the first light of dawn, Barnabas stirred the fire to coax a hot ember into flames to heat water for a tin mug of tea and to warm the last of the hotcakes he had bought while passing through Carlisle. He remembered suddenly that, as he had stepped off the porch of the bakery, a man in buckskins with a crooked nose and a gap of missing teeth had accosted him.

"I take it you are in the trading line of business," the man said, nodding towards the two pack horses lined up behind Little Bay. "Maybe you would like company on the road? My brothers and me are headed west to Fort Pitt, and we could make a little convoy of it. Safer that way, as you might agree." He nodded towards two equally hard-looking men lounging in the saddles of rough-coated horses. One held the reins of another saddled horse.

"I thank you for your offer, friend, but my pack horses are new to the job and we would only slow you down," As he mounted Little Bay, Barnabas spoke civilly. "Good luck to you. Perhaps we'll meet again in Fort Pitt."

The man joined his brothers and tossed over his shoulder through a gap-toothed grin, "And good luck to you." As the three men rode off, Barnabas noted that the horse the man had mounted had a hitch in his stride. Perhaps a loose shoe or an unhealed injury.

Now, Barnabas frowned into his tin mug. He had not liked the looks of the man or his supposed brothers or the condition of the horses they rode. Although they had ridden ahead of him, he had not yet seen them on Forbes Road. A suspicion entered his mind. After tacking up Little Bay and securely arranging the canvas bags and covered rolls of cloth on the pack horses, he led his little pack train to the lip of the swale and paused there while he studied the ground. His suspicion was confirmed. Fresh tracks of three horses, one with an uneven gait, had milled about above his campsite before proceeding west on Forbes Road. His instincts for danger aroused, he opened the flap that held his pistol in place across his chest. One shot against three did not make good odds, but he was adept with his tomahawk, as well.

The road before him rose in a gradual elevation through thick forest. Any bend could conceal an ambush. Barnabas considered the men he had seen in Carlisle. They had not struck him as patient or careful men. If they were setting an ambush, they would not wait long. His horses, laden with trade goods, were tempting targets. The lead line was fastened from his saddle to the halter of the taller horse. The smaller sorrel trotted obediently a few paces directly behind. Little Bay would stop on command. Running through his mind, he played out two outcomes—fight or flee.

Little Bay flicked his ears backward, for the first time annoyed by the horse behind him, who was pulling fractiously against his lead. Prompted to look around, Barnabas saw that the bigger horse was signaling unease, and the smaller appeared ready to bolt. The horses had warned him. He eased the cock back on the pistol inside his coat and brought the tomahawk into his left hand, leaving the reins loose on Little Bay's neck.

In the next instant, Crooked Nose and one of his brothers stepped boldly onto the dusty road; their muskets pointed straight at him.

"Dismount, trader. Give up your goods or die." Crooked Nose smiled his gap-toothed grin. His accomplice whistled through his teeth to alert the third man that their prize was taken. But they were over-confident.

Barnabas leaped wide off Little Bay, crouching as he landed with his pistol already in hand. He fired at once on the Whistler, aiming for the man's black heart, but the shot did not kill the man outright. The impact threw the highwayman off his feet and to the ground, screaming. Crooked Nose brought his musket to bear on his shifting target even as Barnabas instinctively threw his tomahawk. The blade sliced the neck of Crooked Nose and lodged in his collarbone. Both injured men flailed on the ground in agony. Barnabas scooped up the fallen musket and pointed it immediately at the third highwayman as he arrived, still unslinging his musket. Hampered by the reins of three horses, the man was stupidly unready.

Barnabas stared with deadly intent at the man. "I could kill you right now and probably should. Or you can take another way out of this bungled mess. Drop your musket." The man sullenly threw his musket down. "Now, dismount and get your brothers, if they are kin, onto their horses. They might live long enough to reach Carlisle. Anyways, I'll be passing along your descriptions to every fort and post and traveler I pass until I reach the authorities at Fort Pitt."

Barnabas looked with distaste at the writhing Crooked Nose. Stooping over him, he put one foot on the man's chest, braced himself, and, with a snap of his wrist, freed the tomahawk from the bone. Crooked Nose gurgled and passed out. Barnabas threw his kerchief at the third man. "Staunch his blood with that." He inspected the Whistler and found, to his private relief, that the wound had penetrated the soft muscle of the man's upper chest, missing heart and lungs. They both might survive if they didn't bleed to death first. That outcome was up to the third man and their Creator.

Barnabas helped the third man bundle up his brothers securely into their saddles. He sent these nameless scoundrels on their way back to Carlisle, cursing their sorry souls. He kept the three muskets, their powder horns and shot as trade goods to pay him for his inconvenience. Little Bay stood patiently, cropping grass on the verge of the forest road. The pack horses followed suit a little distance away, although the taller flicked an attentive ear as Barnabas approached. He called softly, "Steady on, Patrick. Come along, Henry." As they took tentative steps towards him, Barnabas chuckled. He had given them one distinguished name to share.

TWO

———— + ————

TRADERS AND
TRAITORS

Snug in a corner of raucous Duncan's Tavern, with a plate of hot food and a mug of cider before him, Barnabas relaxed for the first time in many weeks. His horses were stabled for the night, and his trade goods were secured in a warehouse recommended by his supplier. A bed awaited him. By instruction of John Harris, Barnabas dined in this popular meeting place, awaiting an expected contact. He had been advised he would recognize that contact on sight.

Fort Pitt and the town mushrooming around it formed the terminus of all roads, paths, and river routes. Its dirt streets teemed with traders and craftsmen, land speculators and surveyors, spies and scouts, military officers and militiamen, government officials, Indians on tribal business, and prospective settlers heading into the new lands south of the Ohio. Everyone depended on the security afforded by Fort Pitt on the spit of land at the confluence of three rivers—the Allegheny, the Monongahela and the Ohio, all bearing their Indian names. The fort served as the command center for the western field of operations for the Continental Congress and its struggling army.

Barnabas's path led some forty miles north up the Allegheny to the old Delaware town of Kittanning. Mr. Harris had instructed him to supply the trade goods he carried to Jean-Pierre Bellevue, one of Harris's chain of middlemen established at his new trading post on the ruins of the abandoned Delaware town. Patrick and Henry would carry furs and hides back to Harris's Ferry. Unknown to Mr. Harris, Jean-Pierre and Barnabas were old friends.

Gamesters, rolling dice and dropping coins at a nearby table, grew more contentious. Barnabas drew his dinner closer to hand. As expected, the merriment quickly dissolved into a donnybrook of flying fists, threats and curses. He was lifting his mug for a last swallow when one of the combatants was flung over his table, crashing it to the plank floor. At the same moment, a heavy hand descended on his shoulder, and a familiar hoarse voice said, "Time to go, laddie."

In the footsteps of his former sergeant, Barnabas passed through a side door into a stinking alley and through the narrow streets to a small, dimly lit tavern where a few regulars quaffed their evening ale and muttered quietly to one another. Barnabas had been startled to see the sergeant who had set him on this path to Fort Pitt. "It surely wasn't you I was expecting to meet, Sergeant. You're the same fellow who waved goodby to me not three months ago."

"Circumstances change, Corporal. And that's the last time either of us will address the other by rank. Henceforth, you are Barnabas Locke, trader, and I am Joshua Jones, private citizen and land agent." The ex-sergeant paused in thought. "There's a wily fellow who loves injuns in the Ohio Country. He's the white renegade Simon Girty. A turncoat. I see you recognize that name. Girty is a scout and a spy for the redcoats, and he has a seat at just about every council fire to interpret for injuns and redcoats alike. He's been a real thorn in certain sides."

"And just whose sides are those, Mr. Jones?" Barnabas asked. As a newly private citizen devoted to the American cause of liberty, he had undertaken this mission to determine and report on the strengths and allegiances of the Indian tribes of the Ohio Country. He admitted to himself his intense desire to explore those wild lands.

"American sides, Mr. Locke. Simon Girty has proven to be the glue that holds these savages together. He interprets at their councils when they aim to confederate with each other. He's friends with all the chiefs and sachems. He's the interpreter they most trust. And right now, he's been talking plenty against treaties to change the Ohio River as the boundary between injuns only to the north of the river and white settlement in Kentuck to the south. The injuns want to stick us with that border line. The British are telling them to hold on to it because they want the injuns as a buffer between American land and Canada. This Girty has too much influence for one man who is more injun than white. The question we have been sent into these parts to answer is, well, it's 'Where is Simon Girty?' And those who want to know are American men who report to other American men and who pay men like you and me for information."

They discussed their collaboration in this fact-finding mission. Mr. Jones would establish himself in Fort Pitt as a merchant and land agent affiliated with the widely-respected and influential John Harris II of Harris's Ferry. Mr. Jones would serve as a conduit of information regarding the constantly shifting allegiances of the Indian tribes. He would report to John Harris, and Harris would report to his contacts in the chain of influential power brokers. Barnabas would again be eyes and ears in the heart of the frontier.

Barnabas wanted very much to talk with the friend of his youth, Squando, one of the Abenakis who had departed Vermont for the Ohio Country. He had fled the unceasing conflict among the British, the Loyalists, the Americans, the Iroquois, the Algonquins and his own divided Abenaki nation. Squando had a peculiar knack for divining the future. His visions might be very helpful. Barnabas hoped his old friends, the Bellevues, would have word of him.

Early the next morning, after a hearty breakfast, Mr. Jones accompanied Barnabas to retrieve his trade goods and pack train. Once Patrick and Henry were loaded and Barnabas sat astride Little Bay, Jones offered a final word of advice. "Find Simon Girty, but don't turn your back on him."

THREE

WHO IS SIMON GIRTY?

Barnabas, with his little pack train, paused on a bluff overlooking the new settlement of Kittanning, rising from the old Delaware town burned to the ground by American militia. He sighted a few cabins, some tipis indicating Indians in residence, outbuildings and a ferry dock. A ferry boat was crossing from the western bank of the Allegheny to the trading post on the eastern bank. He nudged Little Bay back down onto the path with Patrick and Henry following in single file behind.

He found Jean-Pierre Bellevue at the dock, directing in voluble French the incoming ferry boat to its moorings. Barnabas waited patiently for his old friend to conclude his business with the passengers and to notice his arrival. And when he did, the wiry little Frenchman stared a long moment in disbelief at the whip-thin, dark-haired young man on the bay horse before shouting glad greetings.

"Ah, *mon jeune ami*, climb down from your *petit cheval* so that I may embrace you." Barnabas happily dismounted and allowed his friend to enfold him in his arms. Missus Bellevue hurried down to the dock to add her welcome in Abenaki, to which she reverted when excited. The three friends, followed by the three horses, walked together up the path to the post.

"We have much to talk over, young Barnabas Locke, but first, let us relieve these tired horses from their burdens." His sharp eyes glittered in anticipation.

But Missus Bellevue intervened. "Venison stew is simmering, Barny. You look so thin." She clucked in motherly disapproval. "Take care of your horses, yes, and then we will sit down to a good meal. Business can wait." And she shot a sharp glance at her husband.

With the horses unsaddled and the trade packs stowed, Barnabas was ready to sit down over hot food. The fragrance of fresh-baked bread hung tantalizingly in the air. He was surprised when approaching the broad porch of the post to see a row of five white children dangling their legs over the edge. They dipped thick slices of bread with clean hands into wooden bowls of savory stew. The children looked up from their bowls and, in unison, politely greeted him in French. "*Bonjour, Monsieur.*"

"*Bonjour, mes petits amis*," he responded in kind, wondering how these polite children had come to belong to the Bellevues. It was the first question he asked as he was ushered to the table inside the private quarters of the post.

"They are not ours; more's the pity. They are being returned to their people," Missus Bellevue replied, ladling stew into his bowl.

Responding to Barnabas's interest, Jean-Pierre provided more of the story. "They were captured by warriors of different allegiances from homesteads wrongly established north of the Ohio. To honor the treaty demanding their return, they were escorted here to Kittanning and put into our care. The authorities must find what families are left to reclaim them. I talked long with Simon Girty when he arrived with them. He didn't stay long as he has bad memories of this place. It was here, perhaps you know, years before Armstrong destroyed this town, that his stepfather was burned to death before his eyes, and his mother and brothers were scattered into different tribes. Simon went to the Senecas, where the great chief Guyasuta took him under his wing."

Barnabas munched thoughtfully on a slab of fresh bread as he digested this information, most of which was news to him. It surprised him that Jean-Pierre spoke casually of his meeting with the infamous Simon Girty as though he were merely one of the many frontiersmen who frequented his post on business.

"So, you know Simon Girty?" he asked, gently probing.

Missus Bellevue answered as her husband's mouth was full of bread. "All of us in these western lands come to know Simon Girty. He speaks for the Delawares, the Senecas, the Shawanees, the Wyandots, the Miami, the Potawatomie and for others, too." She laughed and said, "He is learning Abenaki from me. His ear is very quick." In a more serious voice, she added, "He is a good man with a divided soul."

Then the Bellevues remembered as though with one mind that they had important news to relay. Jean-Pierre began the account of what they knew of Squando, the Abenaki. He had been friend and teacher to young Barnabas when he traveled along the Canadian border with his father, the late Frederick Locke, an esteemed trader amongst the Abenaki and Mohawks.

"We have news that will sadden your heart, Barnabas. Your friend and ours, Squando, spoken of as a prophet by many who listen to his visions, is even now imprisoned within the fort at Detroit. It was a horse that was his undoing. You will well remember that high-stepping horse that Squando brought to trade on the very day that the British lieutenant recognized the horse as his stolen mount. Sitting where you sit now, Simon told us what happened at Fort Detroit."

Missus Bellevue cleared away the remnants of the meal and brought mugs of cider to drink while the story was told. The three of them leaned their dark heads together over the table. She began the story.

"Squando had been preaching in a public place outside the fort to Indians who had gathered to hear him speak. He has become eloquent, Barny, and as he reveals his dreams and visions, his hearers can clearly see a future that they do not want. Our beautiful woodlands are no more; the trees are cut to the ceaseless ring of axes, and the air is filled with smoke from many chimneys, not from campfires. Squando foretells a land burdened with white people and empty of our peoples born to this place."

Jean-Pierre picked up the story. "On this day, as he spoke, Squando saw a horse and rider he did not wish to see. But the horse heard his voice and pointed his ears at him and called to him as to an old enemy. His rider turned his eyes to Squando, and they recognized each other in that moment. That rider was the same lieutenant we humiliated before his Hessian soldiers and set adrift in their own boat. Well, you know that part of the story."

Jean-Pierre paused to swig his cider and to collect his thoughts. Speaking so long in English tired his mind. He resumed.

"This British lieutenant, Pembrook, no Pendleton, challenged Squando in that public place. He cried out for all to hear, 'That savage stole my horse and my pistol, too. Arrest him!' Simon Girty was among that crowd gathered to hear Squando speak. He says the officer's voice was shrill with rage. Squando sought to melt away, but British regulars were also on the borders of that crowd and seized him. Squando has been clapped into prison, Barnabas, and Simon Girty tells me his fate is uncertain. Simon stepped forward to speak for this Abenaki, although, as you know, Squando speaks English as well as me. Simon pointed out to McKee, the head of the British Indian Department, that the horse that had been recovered was the very horse Pendleton was riding. The pistol, too, was now recovered as Squando carried it tucked into his sash. There were no grounds to hang any man, not even an Indian, especially one whose people were allied to the British. But the lieutenant was wroth and demanded his revenge. McKee is stalling him, but Simon fears for the Abenaki prophet."

Jean-Pierre finished his cider and sat back in moody silence. Barnabas's mind teemed with the conflicting loyalties presented to him. And yet it seemed clear to him that he could accomplish both his mission and free his friend, God willing, possibly through the unwitting assistance of Simon

Girty himself. Girty was the key to accomplishing both of his objectives.

"Circumstances have changed for me, Jean-Pierre. I think we must talk more about this business of trade." The two men repaired to the storage room of the post to sort out the goods Barnabas had brought on behalf of John Harris. Barnabas set aside small goods easy to carry behind him on Little Bay. He turned over the ledger with relief, the columns already untidy.

"Treat my horses kindly, Jean-Pierre. I hope to return for them when Squando is safe. What can you tell me about this McKee of the British Indian Department?"

Jean-Pierre considered for a moment. "Alexander McKee and Simon Girty and Matthew Elliott left Fort Pitt together when they switched allegiance from the American cause to the British. Simon, I know, felt deeply insulted by the Americans and, even more so, by their secret schemes to take Indian lands both south and north of the Ohio against the terms of all treaties. Powerful interests among the Americans see that land as a way to reward their military and to make land speculators rich. McKee and Elliott are both men of great personal ambition, mercantile men who understand Indian ways and see them as aligned with their interests. These three are great friends, and Girty has been hired by McKee to serve as his most trusted interpreter and scout. They treat with Indians fairly, and, as you have seen with these children on our porch, Simon is quick to protect the lives of innocent people, both white and Indian. A great many untruths have been spread about him."

"I will go to Detroit as fast as Little Bay can carry me. Perhaps by good luck, I will meet with Simon Girty along the way." Barnabas felt the urgency of forming his personal opinion of this man of contradictory reputations. The Bellevues clearly regarded him very differently from the opinions held by Mr. Jones and from the lurid stories widely circulating.

FOUR

MEETING SIMON GIRTY

Barnabas felt unfriendly eyes on him. He had neared the Wyandot town of Upper Sandusky at the headwaters of the Sandusky River but decided to camp at dusk and arrive fresh in the morning with his supply of small trade goods to attract goodwill. Now, he felt the prickle of danger and knew he had made an unwise choice. Little Bay, untacked and hobbled, signaled with his pointed ears that strangers watched from the forest just beyond the grassy little clearing. Barnabas caught small movements among the trees. Had their intent been friendly, the Indians would have already silently arrived to transact business at his campfire. He still wore his coat and under it carried his tomahawk and loaded pistol.

Barnabas made a show of spreading a woolen blanket on the ground and carefully emptying the contents of his tied sacks across it. As he withdrew each item, he held it aloft as though to admire its quality—axeheads, folding knives, ribbons and glass beads, wampum and small musical bells, and other inviting goods. He took for himself a pair of moccasins and slung them about his neck. Then he yawned and stretched elaborately and, with a handful of oats, enticed Little Bay to his side. As the horse lipped the oats from his hand, Barnabas whispered in his ear and then leaned down and swiftly removed the hobbles.

As he rose, he slapped the horse sharply on his rump with a mighty shout. As Little Bay bolted in one direction, he bolted in the opposite. The woods erupted with lithe young figures, some darting after the horse, most pausing to loot the alluring trade goods, and three more seasoned warriors in quick pursuit of the man already many yards ahead of them.

Barnabas chose to run northwest by his best calculation towards his destination of Detroit. Now afoot and pursued, he thought his only chance was to outrun his pursuers until they dropped in exhaustion behind him. He knew himself to be as fleet as any Indian but recognized his handicap of not knowing the terrain. Within moments, he could hear the whoops from the camp as Wyandots scrapped with each other over the trade goods, but far more alarming, the snapping branches of warriors in determined pursuit. He would be their prize.

As dark descended, he relied on his keen night vision to slowly lengthen his lead. He had outrun Indian pursuit before and had confidence it could be done again. He breathed easily, although slapped by branches and thorny underbrush that cut his face and hands. His coat offered some protection but had begun to weigh heavily on his shoulders. He dared not take a moment to fling it aside, for every moment was vital to escape. The terrain was flat and less stony than the woodlands of his upbringing. The trees were not so thickly grown together, and the windfalls were not so tangled. He chanced upon a narrow deer path and thought it might direct him to the Sandusky River, which he hoped to cross to shake off his pursuers.

Their war whoops diminished behind him, but he did not underestimate their Indian persistence. Skilled warriors would not relent easily. Suddenly, the deer trail evaporated from underfoot, and he slid down a steep embankment, free-falling into the fast-moving current of the river. He struggled to keep his head above the water and flailed about for any handhold that would keep him afloat. Debris rushed past him too swiftly to be caught. He was pulled into midstream, blinded by water and darkness, but instinctively began stroking towards the opposite shore. Choking and spluttering, he was entangled by a huge limb that brushed low into the water. Gamely, he thrust his body high enough to latch onto the limb with first one arm and then the other, thereby halting his rapid descent down the river. With the last of his strength, he pulled himself out of the current and over the limb, inching his exhausted body up the limb to the trunk of an ancient tree. He let go and collapsed onto the bank, heaving and retching among the gnarled roots.

Hours later, when he revived, he rolled over and raised his head, listening for sounds of pursuit. He could hear little over the rush of the water below. The sky was brightening, and birds were just beginning their morning conversation. He felt his limbs and torso but found no damage other than the burning slashes across his face, neck, and hands. He wriggled out of his sodden coat, discovering that both his pistol, though soaked, and his tomahawk were still with him. His necessities remained tied to his sash, but the extra moccasins were lost, perhaps even now dangling around the neck of a Wyandot. His first thoughts were to find shelter where he could dry his powder and reload his pistol.

Voices rose from the river. With daylight came renewed pursuit. He peered carefully over the bank and spied two canoes coming fast downstream, one on each side. His pursuers had brought reinforcements, now scanning the banks for his sign. He thanked his good luck that the gnarled limb had been his bridge from the water to the top of the bank, and he had left no sign. And then Barnabas cursed under his breath. The missing moccasins were dangling in plain sight from the same limb that had saved him.

He dodged immediately behind the broad trunk of his tree. He snatched up his wet coat, carrying in its pockets things he would need to survive on foot. He glanced hastily at the ground to make sure nothing was left behind. He ran. A moment later, he heard an exultant shout, and he ran faster.

He fled westward, his mouth dry and his mind working furiously. He calculated the few minutes it would take for his pursuers to beach their canoes, to untangle the moccasins and to find his trail. He disappeared into the dense growth, zigzagging, planting his feet where they would not imprint the mossy earth, running along the tops of fallen trees, laying a false trail and then running up small watercourses, hoping thereby to split the hounds on his trail into two packs. He knew they were experienced trackers, wise to the tricks they had themselves invented.

Suddenly, he was at the edge of a small clearing of high grass. Over his rasping breath, he heard his unshakeable pursuers closing the distance behind him. He hesitated only an instant and then sprang forward. As Barnabas struggled through the waist-high grass, a man astride a roan horse emerged from the forest. In the instant of shocked surprise, Barnabas noticed the two silver-mounted pistols tucked into the red sash around the man's thick waist. Other mounted men, clearly Indian warriors, emerged from the surrounding woods, trapping him exposed in the midst of the clearing.

Instinctively, Barnabas reached for his tomahawk. The man on the roan called out to him in a mild voice, "I assume you are Barnabas Locke?" The mounted men encircled him, a half-dozen muskets aimed at him. The man on the roan, who spoke in clear American, was probably white despite his dark hair, swarthy face, and Indian garb. The others were Indian, of what tribe he could not guess.

"May I ask who is inquiring?" he responded politely, returning his tomahawk to its place on his right hip.

The man urged his horse closer and leaned forward confidentially. "I am Simon Girty, one of those wicked "Injun Girtys" mothers scare their children with at bedtime. People we know in common have put out the word that you desire to meet with me. Well, here I am, young Mr. Locke." He raised his head and straightened in the saddle. "And here, I believe, come the people you are running away from."

Girty was right. The little clearing was suddenly filled with men mounted and on foot. One of the pursuers, notably short but muscular, stepped boldly forth through the tall grass and, in his language, greeted Simon Girty. For some minutes, he spoke passionately, stabbing his finger at Barnabas. Barnabas noted he had a pair of moccasins slung around his neck.

Girty listened respectfully to the warrior and then spoke directly again to Barnabas. "Well, young man, seems like Jim Half-Horse here has put a claim on you. I think I could stake a claim myself. We'll sort it out later. I strongly advise you give me your tomahawk and that pistol." Barnabas felt like a fish between a hawk and a bear. He handed up the weapons to Girty.

Immediately, the warrior seized Barnabas in ownership, binding his wrists behind his back with a leather thong. As another humiliation, he placed a leash around his neck and handed Barnabas over to one of his lieutenants. Within moments, the clearing was empty, and Barnabas was a prisoner of a war party of Wyandots. He had met the infamous Simon Girty.

FIVE

THE GAUNTLET

Word had gone before them. Even before they entered the Wyandot town of Upper Sandusky, a crowd of young and old people had gathered to jeer and taunt Barnabas Locke as he was led like a donkey into their town center. Barnabas, exhausted, hungry, and angry, presented an indifferent, aloof face to his tormentors.

During the day's grueling march at an Indian trot, Barnabas had been punched, shoved, tripped, and kicked back onto his feet. Simon Girty had not intervened. Finally, at a spring where everyone drank and briefly rested, Girty had approached with a gourd of water and lifted it to Barnabas's cracked lips. Quietly, Girty demanded, "Tell me something that will help you." Barnabas had spilled out his story in a torrent of words, only omitting his secret mission as an agent of the Americans. Girty had listened closely but said nothing.

Soon after, Girty had ridden ahead with his entourage of seasoned Wyandot warriors. Likely,

Barnabas imagined bitterly, the renegade Simon Girty was hobnobbing with his Indian friends without a thought for him. He kept alert for Little Bay in case he, too, had been captured, but the horses were corralled beyond the town, and there was no one to ask if he was among them. The thought of never again seeing that brave little horse dispirited him more than his impending trials.

Girty had not forgotten him. Before the war party escorting Barnabas had arrived, Girty had been in negotiations with the Wyandot chief, the town's sachems, and Jim Half-Horse himself. The short, surly warrior had run on ahead to stake his claim. Girty pointed out that it had actually been he and his party of Wyandots who had first encountered Barnabas and held him at musket point before Jim's party arrived at the clearing. He emphasized that they were returning from an official scouting mission on behalf of the British Indian Department in Detroit. Further, he said that the man in question had surrendered his weapons into his, Girty's, hands and didn't that make him Girty's prisoner?

The elders grunted in approval of his reasoning, but Jim Half-Horse vehemently protested it. According to Half-Horse, Barnabas was a trespasser on Indian lands and in contempt of treaty boundaries. Half-Horse and his party had been on his trail since the evening before to exact justice. He had led the pursuit of this miscreant down the river by canoe, had found the evidence of his presence, had tracked him through the forest, and had been on the point of apprehending him when Girty interfered. Furthermore, Girty and his party had stumbled by accident upon the man in the course of other business. What right had he to steal his prize?

When it was again his turn to speak, Girty rose to his feet, paused for a significant moment, and then made a chopping motion with his hand. "What need do I have to steal anything when it falls into my hands? Let us talk about stealing things. Do you not have the young trader's horse in your corral? Are not your womenfolk wearing ribbons and beads and brass bells from his sack of trading goods? Where did you come upon the moccasins you are wearing, Jim Half-Horse? Young Barnabas Locke came in good faith with goods to trade for his safe passage. What is improper in that? He wished to parlay with me and to go with me to Detroit to speak on behalf of the young Abenaki prophet of whom we hear so much. What threat did Barnabas Locke pose, what harm had he done, what insult had he made?" Girty sat down to signify he had finished speaking.

In the Long House, the chief and his sachems deliberated the matter, smoked a pipe together, and eventually arrived at a decision that seemed to them a fair and satisfactory compromise. Girty was pleased with their plan; Jim Half-Horse conceded reluctantly. Barnabas would ride to Detroit on his own horse returned in compensation for his trading losses. Girty would use his influence to assist Barnabas in speaking on behalf of the Abenaki prophet. However, he would be in the custody at all times of either Half-Horse or Girty. The trespassing trader would be turned over to the authorities for ransom to be paid wholly to Jim Half-Horse. All parties agreed that the compromise was contingent upon one vital consideration—that Barnabas Locke must run the gauntlet. People expected as much. Their sense of justice demanded it. His ordeal was set for early the next morning.

While Barnabas hatched hare-brained schemes for escape, Girty had sensibly arranged through diplomacy a rescue of sorts. The disputed prisoner had been deposited, under guard, in the tipi of a middle-aged widow, apparently a medicine woman from the quantity and variety of aromatic herbs that hung from racks and the numerous small clay pots in which she concocted her remedies. Kindly, she bathed the dried blood from his face and hands and applied a soothing poultice to his injuries. She brought him a bowl of stew and a hunk of cornbread to soak up the broth. Barnabas was feeling more optimistic when Simon Girty strolled into the tipi and sat down across from him. The woman courteously provided him with a meal, as well, and then went about her private concerns.

"Mr. Locke, you are going to Detroit. You will have your horse back. You will be held in Detroit for ransom, which is to be paid entirely to Jim Half-Horse. I presume you have someone who will pay it, but I will stand surety until payment arrives. In the meanwhile, you will be in the custody of Jim and me. Jim would be just as happy to take your scalp as take the King's coin, so don't give him cause. Oh, and one other thing. Tomorrow morning, you run the gauntlet."

Barnabas choked on his stew. "The gauntlet?" he questioned in disbelief. "How can I go to Detroit if I'm dead?"

"Try your best not to get dead. I've run it myself, and it ain't a picnic, but you are young and fast. You get through that door to the Long House, and you're a guest of the town until we depart."

"I have a friend, an Abenaki, in prison in Detroit. I know you have already interceded on his behalf. What will happen to him?"

But Simon cut him off curtly in the white man's fashion. "We can talk about Squando later. Tonight, sleep." Before Girty opened the flap, the medicine woman handed him a small pouch with red beads on the tiestring and laid a finger on his lips.

Lulled by the heavy scent of dried herbs and wild flowers, Barnabas sank into a dreamless sleep.

Awakened by the medicine woman, Barnabas prepared himself for his ordeal, tying his moccasin laces tight and stripping himself of his shirt. He mimed to the medicine woman, "Do you have grease?" patting his stomach and shoulders. She immediately recognized his purpose and smiled approvingly. Not only did she smear the grease over his arms and torso, but she urged him to drink a special concoction for what purpose she did not explain. After a few bites to eat and a long swig of water, Barnabas felt as ready as he could make himself. He had no more time for preparation as Jim Half-Horse flung open the flap door and curtly waved him through.

Barnabas blinked in the white light of morning. Seized by his guards, he used his elbows and feet to push away the people crowding aggressively against him. His guards hustled him onto the path leading to the open door of the council's Long House. The people were eagerly jostling into position, shoulder to shoulder in two lines, creating a narrow lane through which he must run. Barnabas took quick note that the young men and older boys had armed themselves with stout poles, the women with sharp switches and thorny branches, and warriors and old men with their war clubs. The door to the Long House seemed an impossibly long distance away. He did not see Simon Girty.

Without warning, Jim Half-Horse pushed him into the fray. Barnabas leaped like a deer. The rain of blows was immediate and furious. He raised his

arms to protect his head and neck, but the pre-
ferred targets were his ribs, his back, his legs, and
knees. He dodged a barrage of thrusts from long
sticks and blows from war clubs. He stomped the
sticks aimed at his feet to knock them from the
hands of his assailants. He brushed close where the
line seemed weakest to deflect blows from falling
with the force of a full swing behind them. Always
another blow found its mark from the other
direction.

The warriors aimed at his torso and lower back,
seeking his kidneys and most tender parts. They
were practiced in their technique to inflict the most
pain possible without killing him too soon. The
women, even those wearing his brass bells, savaged
his face and back with their thorny switches. His
eyes began to swell; his nose seeped blood. The din
of cries and shouts and whoops was tremendous
against his ears. Several times, he stumbled but
instantly recovered his footing and flung his body
forward.

As he neared the end of the gauntlet, he saw
through blurred eyes that Jim's henchmen were
taking up position to inflict punishing blows. Furious, he whirled about, facing the lines of his ene-
mies and thrusting his bleeding arms high into the
air, uttered a sharp cry—an Abenaki war whoop
rivaling in ferocity and defiance any Wyandot yell.
For one brief moment, his opponents were stilled.

In that moment, Barnabas turned back towards the door and . . .

A woman, a very large, angry woman, stood like a rock in the door way of the Long House. Her arms were crossed, and her eyes glittered with cold malice. He countered by dropping abruptly into a crouch, even as blows continued to rain down. As swiftly, she, too, dropped into a crouch to block him. For an instant, their eyes locked, and then Barnabas sprang upward like a cat from his crouch and dove over the woman, even as her grasping hands slid from his greased body. He rolled through the Long House door into sanctuary.

A hubbub erupted outside, but within was a solemn quiet. Several figures moved among motes of smoke and light and took shape as Simon Girty, the Wyandot chief, and the persistent Jim Half-Horse, eager to claim his prisoner should he survive. Barnabas rolled into a sitting position and raised his bloody face towards the figures he could not clearly see. "I thought I would feel more pain," he said in a bemused voice. "I almost feel like laughing."

Simon Girty's rough voice replied through the haze, "Pain is on its way, and so must we be. I've wasted enough time here."

SIX

A FRIENDLY DRINKING GAME

He hurt in every part of his body. Again, Simon Girty had predicted correctly. Jim Half-Horse was constantly at his side, inflicting small miseries. Somehow, Barnabas felt better just having Little Bay beneath him again. The horse sensed that his unsteady rider was in pain and stepped softer. Their party was small—Girty, one of his Wyandot lieutenants named Spybuck, Jim Half-Horse, and Barnabas. Girty had not wasted any time departing Upper Sandusky. Although Barnabas would have done well with a day of recovery, he, too, was fixed on arriving without delay in Detroit. He hoped to consult with Girty regarding Squando's prospects as soon as Girty seemed receptive. At present, he did not.

Late in the afternoon of the second day, already feeling the winds off Lake Erie, they neared Detroit. Girty signaled that they would spend the night at a commonly used campsite. Surprised but relieved that they were not pushing on those last miles, Barnabas wearily dismounted Little Bay. Every muscle ached, but as all of his injuries were superficial, he was already on the mend. Jim Half-Horse was his usual surly self. His boasts and complaints were beginning to wear thin on Girty, but he sweetened the man's temper by suggesting they finish off the small keg of rum he carried in a sack strapped behind his saddle.

Barnabas, tasked with collecting firewood, hobbled like one of the horses. When the sparse meal had been eaten, and the campfire was roaring, Girty uncorked the keg, taking a long, hard swig. He was, by nature, a hard-drinking man. Spybuck passed the keg to Jim Half-Horse, who drank deep and passed the keg back to Girty, pointedly ignoring Barnabas. A teetotaler, Barnabas was primed to make an exception, thinking a swallow or two might be warranted on medicinal grounds. But Girty did not pass the keg to the prisoner. He passed it back to Jim.

Spybuck, who usually remained silent, suggested playing a friendly drinking game. Girty declined to join but offered the remains of his keg to the players. Barnabas was not invited. Spybuck and Half-Horse bore the keg to the other side of the fire, cleared a space in the dirt, and began to toss a pair of dice. The winner of each toss won his opponent's next swig. Surprisingly, Half-Horse won most tosses and was soon in high spirits. Spybuck seemed nonchalant about his losing streak.

Girty turned to Barnabas and asked in a low, conversational tone, "Why are you really in these parts, Barnabas Locke? Why ask for word of where I might be found? Only I found you instead. Are you hoping for the bounty on my head? Are you here to assassinate me?"

Barnabas retorted sharply. "I am not an assassin or a bounty hunter! I have a bounty on my head, too."

Girty persisted. "But why are you here, and not because you want to follow in your father's footsteps? You didn't come to the Ohio Country for that."

Barnabas reconsidered and softened his tone. After all, he did owe his life to Girty. He was not entirely the villain folks made him out to be. However, Jones's advice, "Don't turn your back on Simon Girty," could not be ignored. He decided to answer with part of the truth.

"I wanted to be my own man again. I took an offer to come out here and find answers I hoped would further the American cause, but maybe I'm not so sure about that now. Indians out here are mighty like the Indians I knew growing up. I trust an Abenaki's word over any white man's. You ain't the only man I have known who turned his back on the American cause. One was a young fellow I thought to be my friend, but he was loyal to another cause. And now he's dead. I guess you could say General Arnold's betrayal hit me hard. I rode with that man on the battlefield at Freeman's Farm. He was as brave as any man I ever saw. I got his horse to his feet when they both fell wounded. Right now, I want most of all to get my friend out from under the hangman's noose. Could we talk about that?"

Girty looked satisfied. "We are going to save your Abenaki prophet. His followers are becoming agitated. My employer, Superintendent McKee, would like nothing better than to have him off his hands. That prig of a fellow Pendleton has made a right nuisance of himself. He's creating a brouhaha where none need be. He's a poor excuse for a military man. But, Lord, he does have connections." Abruptly, he seemed to change the subject. "Jim Half-Horse is a nuisance I would like to have off my hands."

Barnabas looked across the campfire. Jim was curled in a ball like a sleeping dog, hugging the empty keg. His snores rose above the crackle of the fire. Spybuck noticed his interest, pocketed his dice, and tossed a little pouch decorated with red beads on the tiestring across the fire into Simon Girty's hands. With the words, "That Indian can't hold his liquor," he smiled wickedly.

Spybuck rolled himself into a blanket and sensibly went to sleep, but Barnabas and Simon talked on quietly. Eventually, Girty yawned, found his blanket, and dropped like a stone into sleep. Barnabas lay awake, aching in body, thinking hard on the topic of allegiance and what it meant to other men and himself. He fell asleep without coming to any conclusions.

Jim Half-Horse woke to the bright light of mid-morning. His mouth was a fiery furnace, his eyes bloodshot, and his head felt split open. Spybuck, looking none the worse for the drinking game, was scattering the ashes of last night's fire. Their horses stood saddled and ready. A stack of silver coins rested atop the empty keg. Jim's prisoner and Girty were gone.

SEVEN

---·---

AMBUSH

"Jean-Pierre Bellevue spins a good yarn. Told me one about the Prophet and you and a British horse that had me in a knot. But it made a British lieutenant thirsty for vengeance. I think maybe only your death or imprisonment will slake that thirst. He won't be listening to reason when it comes to you, but he might listen if there's something he wants even more than revenge. What might that be?"

Barnabas figured he was being tested. What would a British lieutenant want more than revenge after being held up to ridicule, robbed of his boots and his horse, and then his pistol and his sword, demoted, and exiled to a posting at the ends of the earth? From Pendleton's point of view, Barnabas recognized that he had inflicted great harm on that tetchy young officer. One idea did occur to him.

"To be promoted to a captain?" he tentatively suggested to Simon Girty, who nodded in pleased approval. "Maybe to be posted as a captain to Montreal or some place grander than Detroit?"

"That would stop the sniggers when he passes. That would put him back into the civilized world. But what would get him the three stars of a captain? And how do we make that so? Trickery, I guess," said Girty, shrugging his shoulders as he answered his own question.

"Jim Half-Horse must have woke powerfully mad this morning. Will he be on our heels?" Barnabas asked.

"Likely Spybuck has persuaded Jim that he can be a hero in his home town, coming back so quick with the ransom money to lord it over his mates," Girty responded without much interest. "Though short, he makes a big noise."

As the miles dwindled toward Detroit, they passed others bound for the British stronghold, some of them hailing Girty by name. Barnabas considered that he might have no better opportunity to pick Girty's mind than right now. Maybe Girty was pondering the same question because he said something, as though speaking his thoughts aloud before Barnabas could speak.

"It seems that a lot of futures depend on the truth of your Abenaki's prophecies. He does not paint a pretty picture—trees all felled for cabins and barns and planting crops. No bison or elk or skies dark with pigeons. I talked to your friend about his visions. He believes in 'em. Has seen the same in his own country." Barnabas nodded his agreement. White settlers had swept into the Green Mountains and beyond to the Canadian border even while the war raged in the South. Squando had chosen to take his chances in the Ohio Country. Then, Girty added an odd remark.

"Your friend made a prophecy about me, which I don't much like and damn well hope is wrong."

It was dusk when they rode into the narrow streets of Detroit. Mist rose from the river and chilled the air. Barnabas longed for a hot meal and a warm bed. They stabled the horses at a livery that rented Girty private space with a door that could be locked on the floor above the stalls. They dropped their saddles and bedrolls there and washed up from a basin. Girty removed his worn Indian traveling clothes and assumed his town attire—with the two silver-mounted pistols tucked into his red sash. Barnabas noted that his tomahawk hung from the sash at the middle of Girty's back but made no comment. He gazed longingly at one of the narrow bunks but followed the indefatigable Girty out again into the thickening fog.

Girty knew the tavern where he would most likely find Superintendent Alexander McKee. Like Girty, McKee enjoyed the camaraderie and conversation that flowed with good liquor. Many a nugget of useful gossip was picked up here, along with the usual rumors and wild fabrications. The tavern, near the end of a long street along the riverbank, put Barnabas in mind of rowdy Duncan's Tavern in Fort Pitt. He hoped no one would be flung over his meal tonight. A fiddler sawed away at a lively tune Barnabas recognized with amusement. It was what the Americans called "Yankee Doodle Dandy."

As Girty predicted, they found McKee dining convivially with friends at a table in a nook near the fireplace. McKee rose immediately from the table, made his excuses to his associates, and joined Girty and Barnabas at a smaller table in a quieter corner.

"So, I've been waiting for you to show up, Simon. Your runner informed me you were delayed on unexpected business at Upper Sandusky," and here McKee looked at Barnabas. "This is your latest rescue, is he? He looks mighty ragged."

Barnabas, although somewhat offended, seized the moment. "Sir, I'm here in Detroit to rescue my good friend if rescuing is necessary. You know him as Squando, the Abenaki Prophet."

Girty raised his hand and said, "Later, Locke. I've got business with the Superintendent here." The two old friends, who had abandoned the American cause the same night, bent their heads together while Girty gave McKee his verbal report.

Barnabas listened closely, trying not to appear so. Much of what Girty had to say about recent events along the Ohio River was useful information, but Barnabas had no way at present of relaying his report to his superior. He was uncomfortably aware of that prickling sensation of being watched. Everyone in the tavern appeared engaged in conversation or serious lonely drinking or flirting with the serving wenches. But one scruffy fellow, in a waterman's clothes, sat alone at the least hospitable table, right inside the doorway where every opening of the door blew cold fog into the tavern. That man was taking an interest in the three men at Girty's table.

After an interminable time in parlay with Girty, McKee rose. "I'm off for home. The missus will wonder what's become of me. Come by the Department mid-morning tomorrow. I'll have your report written out for signature. And you can pick up your reimbursement for the ransom you paid for this one," and the Superintendent turned slightly towards Barnabas. "We can look into the Squando affair then. My prisoner is just as much a nuisance to me as yours is to you, Simon."

Barnabas felt more like an accomplice than a prisoner. He wondered without much interest whether Mr. Harris, who had given him a line of credit, would pay the Indian Department for Girty's silver coins left on the small keg. Girty wanted to stay and drink, but Barnabas refused to drink with him. His head was already thumping. He felt again the draft of the opening and closing door and glanced over.

The waterman was gone. Immediately, he knew it was time for Girty and himself to be gone, as well. He had forgotten how much Girty was worth to the Continental Congress, a one thousand dollar bounty collectible by anyone who could deliver him to American authorities.

Pleading his poor state, Barnabas urged Girty to pay the tab and then hurried him through the gauntlet of cronies and hangers-on who reached out for a word with the popular, notorious "Injun Girty." Eventually, they passed through the tavern door into a night of heavy fog and drizzling rain.

Barnabas said softly into Girty's ear, "I think we are walking into an ambush. Are your pistols primed?" He slipped his left hand under Girty's sash and retrieved his tomahawk. Girty did not object. For all his hard-drinking, his mind was, as always, alert to danger.

Instinctively, both men felt in their bones where an ambush could be laid at the turning of the long street from the riverside into the warren of dark, narrow streets they had navigated earlier that evening. When the dark shapes of five men fell upon them with cudgels and belaying pins as they turned that sharp corner, they were already mounting a defense. Girty held both cocked pistols at the ready and discharged one at a figure lunging out of the fog. That figure fell instantly to the wet ground. Barnabas deflected the downward thrust of a belaying pin with his tomahawk, simultaneously kneecapping the man and taking him writhing to the ground. Barnabas spun away from a second attacker, narrowly avoiding a cudgel aimed at his head. He brought his knee up sharply into the man's groin while bringing the blade of his tomahawk down across his forearm. The man dropped the cudgel and doubled over, screeching in pain.

Barnabas spun about looking for Girty and saw him lay his unspent pistol against the chest of an assailant, stopping him in his tracks. Girty flipped the spent pistol in his other hand and smacked the butt cap hard against the ruffian's temple. He dropped like a stone. The fifth man, possibly the waterman who had alerted his confederates, abandoned the fight.

Barnabas breathed hard, adrenaline pumping through his veins. Strangely, the suddenness of the attack exhilarated him, the danger that came out of the dark and wet, the grunting and cursing of men in close mortal combat. He was profoundly relieved that his instincts remained sharp and by the speed of his reflexes. He had met Death and rebuffed it. At his feet, three men lay prone, a fourth was scrambling away on his hands and knees, and the fifth had disappeared into the night.

Girty seized Barnabas by the arm. "Let's get the hell out of here," he hissed. "This scum will only bring more scum."

EIGHT

THE SQUANDO AFFAIR

Barnabas lay with open eyes the next morning, thinking hard and waiting for Girty to awake. The man slept in unnerving quiet. Had the Senecas taught him not to snore or move in his sleep, Barnabas wondered. Suddenly, Girty was awake and on his feet. The first words out of his mouth stunned Barnabas.

"Your prophet got it nearly right last night. He warned me twice against an attack with a sword from behind in the dark. Well, I expect he may have seen a sword where I saw a cudgel, but it's much the same if it's being swung at your head."

Barnabas was surprised that Girty's fate had prompted warning visions by his friend. He guessed that Girty was the sort of fellow who would invade any man's dreams. Thinking about last night, he realized again that his life had also been in danger. Yet Squando's vision, as reported to Girty, did not include Barnabas in the midst of that ambush.

Before breakfast, Girty directed them to a wash house, where they shed the stink and grime of long days of travel. While Barnabas soaked in the tub of steaming water, the knots in his bruised muscles relaxing, the wash house attendant brushed his clothes as clean as he could get them, rubbed at the blood stains, and stitched several tears closed. At Girty's suggestion, he tendered a small brown jar of ointment for Barnabas to treat his cuts and scrapes. "It works on horses, too," the man helpfully informed him.

Cleaned up and fed, they took crowded streets toward the fort, the sentries waving Girty and his companion through the gates, and turned smartly into the long, low building housing the British Indian Department. In his office, Deputy Superintendent Major Alexander McKee awaited them, lifting the quill from the document lying before him on his cluttered desk.

"You arrive in good time, gentlemen," he greeted them heartily. "My draft is ready for review." As soon as they were seated, McKee launched into the reading of the report Simon had dictated to him in the tavern. Simon voiced a few corrections, suggestions which McKee scribbled down. When they were both satisfied, McKee called for his secretary to put the draft into a fair copy for signatures. The report would be sent on to McKee's superiors. It passed through Barnabas's mind that Simon Girty could not read or write, although he could recall a speech in any language word for word.

Barnabas listened attentively, storing into his capacious memory the details of names and locations. The thrust of the report was that the Indians, with few dissensions, were uniting against any change to the Ohio River as the boundary line between the hunting grounds of Kentucky, already nearly lost to white settlement, and the Ohio Country to the north of the river and still salvageable. They demanded that the British keep them supplied with guns and ammunition, with provisions and food stock for the winters, as the united tribes stood as a buffer between the land-hungry Americans and the British in Canada.

"Before we discuss your matter, young man," McKee said, turning towards Barnabas, "new business has come before me. Soldiers on patrol picked up four river men in a pretty poor state, two of them outright dead. We're looking for a fifth man." He tapped his finger on the desk. "The ones who lived say they were attacked by Indians, unlikely as that sounds. One of them sports the slash of a tomahawk on his arm. So, Commandant Major De Peyster has dropped the matter into the lap of the Indian Department. Is this matter any affair of yours?"

Girty shrugged noncommittally. Barnabas replied, "Mr. Girty has my weapons." He really did not want to be embroiled in this new complication. To what end? McKee supplied the answer.

"The two ambushers who can talk have already talked plenty. The fifth man will give up the name of their ringleader. Possibly that of a British officer. Should the officer under suspicion be someone known to you both, perhaps even more so to Mr. Locke, then the Indian Department and Commandant De Peyster see a path to solving our twin problems—my Abenaki Prophet and his inept British lieutenant. It appears no money was exchanged, but the promise of bounties on your heads to be delivered by both sides in this war with the Americans has been dangled as a rich reward for murder."

Girty leaned forward in his chair, his quick mind seizing upon the possibilities. If proof of incitement to murder could be laid at Pendleton's feet, the Commandant could induce his lieutenant to drop the charges against Squando. The enticement of a captaincy would surely clinch the deal. De Peyster would insist on a reposting of this troublesome lieutenant and McKee on the banishment from the Ohio County for the equally troublesome prophet.

Barnabas had nearly forgotten that the British had posted a bounty on his head. That had been more than three years ago when he ventured north as a spy from Fort Ticonderoga. Yet that bounty might be his undoing.

"Now, can I see Squando the Abenaki, your prisoner and my friend?" he asked with a shade of testiness in his voice.

McKee amicably agreed and rose to escort Barnabas to the stockade at the far end of the headquarters of the Indian Department. Girty had business elsewhere. As they strode down the long porch fronting the building, McKee mentioned casually to Barnabas, "Your Indian friend seems to be in poor appetite." While a sentry unbolted the heavy doors of the holding cell, Barnabas abruptly confronted McKee before he stepped through. "I hope you intend to let me out of there." McKee assured him that this was no trick. "Tell Squando the terms of our agreement, but make it clear that his release depends on Pendleton. Tell him that he must depart the Ohio Country forever." Barnabas stepped through, and the door thudded behind him.

His eyes adjusted to the dimness of the room, lit by only a few narrow slots high in the rough timber walls. The dirt floor was covered in grimy sawdust. A bucket of dank water hung just inside the door. Another full of human waste stood in a corner. The room stank.

Here was Squando approaching him in disbelief. His handsome face was haggard, and his muscular body was too thin. He spoke in Abenaki. "How have you come here, Barny? Are you captive? I have seen no visions concerning you." Usually, in calm command, Squando struck Barnabas as in serious distress.

"No, no, Squando. I am here with a plan to release you. Let us sit here while I explain." Squando was one of a small number of Indians, most apparently sleeping off drunkenness, another two playing a desultory game of dice. Barnabas did not doubt that they were all listening. He, too, spoke in Abenaki.

"Simon Girty has talked with Superintendent McKee." He explained what he knew of their plan, although he guessed Girty and McKee had kept details from him. "However," and here Barnabas drew a deep breath, "success depends on Pendleton. I believe he will rise to the bait. He will take his fancy horse and go to some posting at Montreal or Niagara as a captain. You and me will leave the Ohio Country and this tangle of greed and killing and go west of the Mississippi into Spanish territory. You have made yourself a thorn to the authorities in these parts, Squando, though you have only spoken your truths. I find myself in league with the infamous Simon Girty and not much bothered by it. Neither of us have obligations to keep us here. We are for the West together, Squando. Agreed?"

Squando looked long into the earnest face of his friend. "Our fates seem sealed as if we are brothers by blood. My visions stir only anger and fear, and I would happily be rid of them. My people have scattered, and I have no place to call home." He clasped his friend's hand in both of his. "We go west. It is agreed."

Then Squando looked pointedly at the pouch Barnabas carried over his shoulder. "Do I smell pork in there?" he asked. Barnabas hastily pulled out a packet of fried pork and cornbread wrapped in greased paper purchased that morning with Squando in mind. As Squando devoured the food, Barnabas recounted the ambush of last night. "That surely convinced Girty of the power of your visions." Squando swallowed a mouthful of cornbread, thought for a moment, and then said, "Tell Girty he is still in danger from one he trusts. It was a sword I saw over his head."

NINE

APPLES

A silent sentry escorted Barnabas back to the Superintendent's office and deposited him in the secretary's anteroom to await McKee's return. Barnabas felt confident that he and Squando would soon be on their way to Spanish territory. First, he had a mission to honor. He found what he was looking for still on the secretary's desk, lying beside a pot of ink and sharpened quills—the draft in the Superintendent's clear hand—and smoothed out the wrinkles. He read the pages over quickly, noting again the scrupulous detail with which Girty had provided his report. At the bottom, he penned a line of provenance and, to identify himself as the sender, a phrase in Latin, maybe misspelled, but he knew it would be recognized only by the recipient.

Barnabas found a sheet of heavy good paper and folded and sealed his packet, stamping it with McKee's official stamp. He addressed the outer page with a flourish to Joshua Jones, Esq., Land Agent, in care of Duncan's Tavern, Fort Pitt. He thrust his missive deep into the mail pouch hanging on its hook inside the door. For four years, he had served in the Rangers as a courier, and the sight of that mail pouch earlier in the day had sparked the idea. Mail got delivered. Pleased with himself, he walked nonchalantly down the hall and stepped outside under the overhang of the long porch.

Even in the heat of mid-afternoon, the parade ground was busy with foot traffic and the occasional mounted officer trotting through the gates. He saw Indians in their best attire, men of the frontier in buckskins, soldiers and civilians, all of them occupied with the business of the day. He stepped off the porch to help a laundress, a servant of African descent, whose basket had tumbled off her hip, spilling bed linens on the hard-packed earth. She thanked him, and as he straightened up, he met the murderous blue eyes of one Lieutenant Pendleton, striding towards him as though to strike him to the ground, with his hand clenching the hilt of his sword.

Barnabas smiled tightly into the angry face and saluted him briskly. "So, our paths cross again, Lieutenant Pendleton. I am, as you see, unarmed and a guest of the Superintendent." Nevertheless, Barnabas backed up onto the porch to give himself the advantage of the upper ground.

A flow of virulent words spewed from the lieutenant as he looked up at Barnabas standing at ease above him. "I'll see you dead before I'm done with you, Barnabas Locke. You and that Abenaki dog! You scoundrel, you, you stole my horse, my sword, my pistol, my coins and tried to steal my honor as an officer and a gentleman."

"Oh, let's not forget the boots and buttons, Lieutenant," Barnabas goaded him from the safety of the porch. "At least you are not being demoted again but promoted against all reason to captain."

"I knew you were at the bottom of this conspiracy. Everyone, even Commandant De Peyster, takes the part of that Abenaki charlatan. I despise him, and you are nothing but a deserter with a bounty on his head. By God, I'll have that bounty or your head!"

"And you, sir, are at the bottom of the scurrilous attack against me and Simon Girty this night past. You might well look to your own neck. Consider this a good day that you are not clapped into the stockade." Barnabas was hot with rage.

A sly thought occurred to the lieutenant. He drawled out his words with a self-satisfied smirk. "I know a very pretty apple orchard in Vermont. Perhaps I should pay it a visit."

Before the officer could utter another word, Barnabas leaped off the porch and onto the lieutenant. They tumbled together to the ground, thrashing and punching wildly at each other until Barnabas had the lieutenant pinned beneath him. He slapped the smirking face, first with the palm of his hand and then with the back.

"If you harm one apple on my uncle's farm, you lobster-backed bastard, I'll . . ." but two pairs of strong hands tore him off the lieutenant and yanked them both to their feet. "At attention, Lieutenant!" McKee roared.

McKee turned on Girty, "No more delay. I want that Indian and your pup out of Detroit at once." He turned contemptuously to the lieutenant. "And you, rolling on the ground in public like a common brawler. You are a disgrace to your uniform. Take yourself off to Niagara on your ten-day leave. The Commandant wants you out of his sight!"

Pendleton choked back the furious words on his tongue, made a show of brushing the dust from his sleeves, then spun about and marched rigidly across the parade ground.

Girty seized Barnabas by the arm and briskly walked him away. He was weary of the whole business, but he was curious enough to ask, "What the hell was that all about?"

"Apples, just apples," Barnabas replied shortly.

Girty got down to brass tacks. "Now, Barnabas Locke, it's time for you to collect your prophet and leave the Ohio Country for good. Your horses are saddled at the livery. Squando leaves today in broad daylight for all to see at liberty. That should appease his followers. Spybuck and his warriors will meet you and Squando. They will give you protection until you are well away from Detroit. From there, you are on your own." He withdrew Barnabas's pistol from his shoulder bag. "Your pistol. You will likely need it."

Barnabas tucked the pistol into his belt and asked politely, "Isn't there something else you want to return?"

"Oh, yes," and Girty reached an arm behind his back. He hefted Barnabas's tomahawk approvingly before handing it to his erstwhile prisoner. "It's a nice weapon."

Barnabas was cooling down. "I thank you, Mr. Girty, for all that you have done to help me and Squando. You have acted the part of a friend, although we are not friends on the same side of this war. I know you think Squando's vision concerning you has been fulfilled, but he thinks not. He said it was a sword he saw over your head."

"Take care of yourself, Barnabas Locke, and I'll take care of men wielding swords. Here, take these, some coins to grease your way." He took a small pouch from his sash, pressing it into Barnabas's hands despite the young man's protests. He clapped Barnabas on the shoulder heartily and walked swiftly away, muttering, "Apples, he says."

TEN

SQUANDO SPEAKS

They made a show of leaving Detroit. Someone, probably Girty or McKee himself, had alerted
Indians of influence to escort, with all due respect
their Abenaki Prophet from the town. Squando
was mounted on a saddled gray horse, rumored
among the crowd to be compensation for his weeks
of detention in the stockade. The gray had little
spirit left within his old bones.

In the shade of trees, Barnabas, astride Little
Bay, awaited his friend. Uncomfortably, he felt
again that prickling sensation of being watched.
He scanned the growing crowd preceding Squando's arrival for a pair of eyes turned towards him.
At the distance of a musket shot, he spied what he
half-expected to see. Lieutenant Pendleton, almost
unrecognizable out of uniform, was staring directly
at him over the pointed ears of a horse Barnabas
knew well and had once called Macaroni for his
fancy looks. He watched as four large men on

rangy horses fell in with the lieutenant. "Hah," Barnabas thought, "Pendleton has recruited his escort of armed men." By the military cast of them, Barnabas suspected they were Hessians, dangerous mercenaries and free agents no longer employed by the British Army.

Squando, accompanied by his entourage of Indians, arrived to a great shout of welcome and dismounted. He stood tall as he raised his hand to signal he would speak. The crowd went quiet. Squando spoke in a voice pitched to the outer circle of his listeners, but that voice was resonant and measured. Barnabas listened attentively.

"My friends, the authorities have told me not to speak to you anymore about my dreams, my visions, my picture of the life that is coming upon us. They say my truths make you angry, make you fearful, make you skeptical of their promises. So, I will not speak of the future. I will speak of the present, of what my eyes see and my ears hear. We are many peoples—Shawnee, Delaware, Wyandot, Miami, Potawatomi, Huron, Seneca, and many others. A few Abenaki, too, have come among you, fleeing the white settlers of our home country. The white people call us all "Indians." They do not respect us. They try to buy our allegiance for their purposes as they fight their endless wars amongst themselves. White people believe they can buy anything, even men and women, even the land itself.

We are people of the land. The land is our mother, and we honor her. When the land tells us we press too hard upon her, that she cannot breathe, then we leave our villages and our cornfields. We go where the land is full of game, and the rivers are full of fish. The great hunting grounds of Kentucky, where your ancestors hunted for bison and elk and deer and where they gathered salt and reaped the bounty of the forests, the rivers and the skies dark with passing birds, are being lost to all of the people of the land.

The white people first came to our lands in the hundreds, then in the thousands, and now in the many thousands. All of them desire only one thing—land. Land is the measure of their lives. They will barter those lives for land. They decide who owns the land with writing on paper. Is this natural? They come with axes and saws and cut down the trees to make fields for farms. They work the land until it cries out for rest, but they do not listen to their mother. Is this natural? They work their women and children and leave them unprotected without laughter or companionship while the men work alone in their fields. Is this natural? The ways of the white people are not the ways of the people of the land. I see what I do not wish to see, but I will say no more. I bid you all farewell."

Upon his conclusion, the throng paused for a long, respectful moment and then surged forward to embrace him and wish him a good journey. Several approached with gifts—a pair of moccasins, a blanket roll, a water gourd, a tomahawk acquired in trade, and provisions for the journey. One warrior of advanced age gifted the young Prophet with a strongly made bow and a quiver full of arrows. Barnabas heard his short speech bestowing the gift. "I hunted meat and my foes with this bow. My father instructed me in the making of it when I was a boy growing into manhood. I protected my wife and my children with this bow. Now, I have no wife. Now I have no sons living. Take this bow and these arrows, and may they keep you safe from hunger and from evil men." Barnabas wondered at the spontaneous generosity of these people.

The two friends rode side by side westward, Barnabas urging them onward at a fast pace as he told Squando of Pendleton in civilian clothes and in the company of four rough men of suspicious intent. "You always underestimated that officer, Barny. You thought him a joke, and he deeply resents you. That he pays four men to kill us tells how much he wants us dead. And I will tell you something you may not have seen. Those men are armed with Jaeger rifles." At Barnabas's dismayed expression, Squando smiled slightly and said, "I have spies, too, Barny."

ELEVEN

SACRED GROUNDS

At dusk, Girty's seasoned scout Spybuck and two of his trusted comrades quietly emerged out of the darkening forest. Barnabas recognized both of these warriors from the beating he took as he ran the gauntlet just a few days ago. His body bore their bruises. Now, these Wyandots would be a powerful deterrent to any attack against him. He relayed what he knew of Pendleton's probable intentions, to which Spybuck grunted an acknowledgment. Soon after, a young Wyandot rode up from behind and brought his horse alongside Spybuck. He was one of their party, a warrior in the making named Red Hand, stationed behind to watch their rear. He confirmed that five well-armed men were riding on their trail. Pendleton's threats had not been idly made. His hired, highly trained Hessians outgunned the Wyandots.

Spybuck called a halt. "Five men are riding fast behind us. When they see our tracks join yours, they will know that they are in pursuit of six men, not two. This is not to our advantage." He instructed two of his warriors to circle back through the forest to flank the mercenaries, one on either side of the trail, well hidden in the forest. He put his young recruit, Red Hand, to the task of brushing their horses's tracks from the trail. Pendleton's mercenaries would guess that their quarry had been joined by only two others, perhaps allies or fellow travelers going in the same direction.

"We have muddied the waters. I suspect they will send one of their party ahead to reconnoiter our numbers and our strength," Spybuck opined.

Barnabas said, "I am always the one falling into ambushes. I would like to set one myself." There were nods in agreement.

They pressed on until the last glimmers of light. Encamping on a site just off the trail, well used by travelers, they built a large fire so that any interested party would plainly see four men and their horses. They spoke among themselves loudly and retired to their bedrolls only when the fire had died to embers. In turn, each of them slipped from his bedroll and kept watch on the trail. On the last watch, under changeful moonlight, Barnabas, perched in the large limbs of a chestnut tree, saw below him a stealthy figure on foot moving up the trail. A metal gorget glimmered around his neck. Barnabas went very still in his tree, training his night eyes on the man as he crept to the outer circle of their camp, counting the bedrolls and the horses tethered nearby. After a long moment, the silent scout returned into the night. Spybuck had rightly called Pendleton's strategy. The scout would report four men.

Before slipping back into his plumped-up bed-roll, Barnabas softly made his report to Spybuck, who merely grunted, turned over and went back to sleep.

The party of four rode together through the next morning over terrain that merged gradually from forest to grasslands until they arrived on the banks of a small tributary of the Sandusky River. They made a show of a friendly parting. Spybuck and the young Red Hand crossed the tributary towards Upper Sandusky and rode far enough to lay a false trail. They would double back, disguising their tracks in high-grass marshland that crossed the faint trail ahead. Then, they would recross the little tributary farther down to rejoin the American and the Abenaki at an agreed-upon landmark. A tree-topped mound, held sacred as a burial ground for a nameless people, rose above the open grassland, dotted with the droppings of bison that wallowed and grazed in this flat river valley. Ideal as the site for an ambush, the mound would provide cover in open country and high ground for marksmen to train their weapons on riders exposed in the grassland below. Spybuck had chosen well.

But in these short unprotected miles was the vulnerability in their plan to lay an ambush at the mound. If Pendleton remained unaware of the two silent Wyandots flanking him and bought the ruse of the parting at the tributary, then now was the lieutenant's best chance to catch his quarry. The pursued young men rode alert for the drumming of hoofbeats coming up fast behind them. Squando grasped his strung bow and two arrows in one hand. Barnabas checked the priming of his pistol. They picked up the fastest pace Squando's gray horse could sustain.

Spybuck had estimated the grassy mound to be about five miles from their parting point at the little tributary. As their rendezvous rose into sight, Barnabas and Squando believed they had successfully outpaced their pursuers. But they had miscalculated. Casting a glance over his shoulder at Squando, kicking his tiring gray, Barnabas saw in the distance the unmistakable bright chestnut horse ridden by Lieutenant Pendleton. He was galloping boldly towards them, followed by the four Hessians and gaining ground with every stride. "Damn him to hell," Barnabas cursed the man he had yet again underestimated. He saw with fear one of the Hessians raise and sight his deadly accurate Jaeger rifle on the tempting target of Squando on his failing horse.

A rifle shot barked. Barnabas spun Little Bay about as the old gray stumbled to the ground.

Squando rolled away but rose immediately and notched an arrow in one fluid motion. He brought the bow to its full draw and sent the arrow, followed instantly by the other, into the chest of the nearest Hessian bearing down upon him. Pendleton, on his chestnut, flashed past Squando, intent only on Barnabas.

As Barnabas launched Little Bay toward the oncoming Macaroni, the two horses brushed solidly against each other. Little Bay squealed and kicked out against Macaroni's flanks. The chestnut stumbled, unseating Pendleton. Wheeling Little Bay about, Barnabas threw his leg over his horse's neck in a flying dismount, landing with his pistol in hand, facing Pendleton as the lieutenant regained his feet.

In the space between the two men, in a sudden frenzy of animosity, the horses reared against one another, feinting, biting, kicking, and raising a screen of dust. Little Bay, faster and more agile, dodged Macaroni's savage teeth and hooves and landed kicks solidly against the chestnut's ribcage. When Macaroni had had enough and bolted, Little Bay pursued, sinking his teeth into the glossy chestnut rump and biting off a hank of tail.

As the dust settled, Barnabas and Pendleton stood face to face on the trail, much as they had stood four years ago on the shore of Lake Champlain. Pendleton sneered as he aimed his pistol at

Barnabas's heart. But Barnabas was not cowed and did not lower his pistol, his finger resting on the trigger.

"This time, my Hessians have their rifles aimed squarely on you, Barnabas Locke. You will never dishonor me again."

But the lieutenant's triumph was premature even though three ruthless mounted Hessians backed him. From his viewpoint on the trail, Barnabas watched two Wyandot warriors closing swiftly. His visible relief alerted the lieutenant, who sharply turned his head and saw Barnabas's reinforcements nearly upon them. "Shoot them!" he shouted in a high pitch. "And you," he addressed the Hessian wearing the gorget around his neck, "you shoot that Abenaki dead." As the Hessians wheeled about in a flurry of horseflesh and raised their weapons, two more shots cracked the air. Spybuck and Red Hand emerged from the gun smoke on the mound above. Two Hessians, mortally struck, tumbled from their mounts. The third spurred his rangy horse about into a fast gallop as two Wyandot warriors whooped in close pursuit, passing the three men still standing on the plain below the mound.

Suddenly alone in his vendetta against Barnabas, his paid mercenaries either dead or deserted, and even his horse galloping away, Pendleton remained intent on revenge against his wily nemesis. He smiled thinly as he pulled the trigger of his pistol. Bullet and smoke belched outwards. In that instant of smoke and sound, followed by the searing passage of the bullet through his side, Barnabas faltered backward, his pistol undischarged, dangling from his hand. When he raised it again, Pendleton's empty pistol, thrown like a war club against his head, struck his left ear, and everything went dim and muted.

By the time Barnabas had regained his senses, Pendleton had already seized the reins and mounted one of the milling Hessian horses. He aimed the horse like a weapon straight towards him. As Barnabas dodged the horse, Pendleton's booted foot to his chest knocked him to the ground. He watched in fury as the lieutenant wheeled his horse away. Yet even as he tasted sour defeat, his most trusted ally halted at his side. Little Bay had faithfully returned, and in his wake followed the bright chestnut Macaroni.

Ignoring the burning in his side, he vaulted onto Little Bay. He shouted to Squando, limping towards him, that he was in pursuit of the fast-disappearing Pendleton. Squando snared the bridle of the fractious Macaroni, hauled himself into the saddle, and rode after them.

Barnabas caught up with Pendleton on the banks of the little tributary. The Hessian's horse was refusing to cross the water, and Pendleton was beating him with the flat of his short sword. The horse sensed that this was an unsafe crossing, alerted by the suspicious swirls of water in an otherwise calm flow. Compelled by the urgency of his rider, the horse slid down the bank into belly-high water and then stubbornly balked. He whirled about and tried to scramble back up the slippery bank. The strained girth strap parted, and the saddle and rider were thrown backward into the water. Pendleton disappeared beneath the surface.

Frantic to be finished with him, Barnabas leaped off Little Bay, slid down the bank and into the water after the lieutenant. He held his primed pistol above his head. His eyes searching for a sign of the submerged man, Barnabas saw the glint of sharp, shining metal rising from the rippling water. He watched, mesmerized by its ascent, followed by Pendleton's head, thrown back, his open mouth gasping for air. His body rose, almost in slow motion, to the level of his chest, with his upheld right hand holding his sword above his head. They were face to face yet again with only a few feet of water between them, Pendleton's blue eyes wide and wild with murderous intent. Uttering a piercing cry, he abruptly brought his right hand down and thrust the sword towards Barnabas. Without hesitation, Barnabas leveled his pistol and pulled the trigger. Pendleton's face registered stark surprise as he fell back into the swirling water.

As Barnabas struggled up the muddy bank, Pendleton's body drifted into mid-current and was caught by a whirlpool. The men on the bank watched in silence, Barnabas dripping water and blood and Squando sitting with an injured leg stretched out before him.

Spybuck offered to retrieve Pendleton's body. It was dangerous to leave it exposed for discovery, and it might drift downstream to Upper Sandusky, raising the alarm. The man was unpopular but well-connected. There would be questions when he did not show up after his ten-day leave. Spybuck put Red Hand in charge of the retrieval as part of his education. When the body lay on the bank, Spybuck said to Barnabas, "Your kill, your scalp."

Barnabas shuddered slightly, perhaps from the cold wetting, but declined. "No, I've taken many things dear to him in his life. I'll send him to the hereafter with his hair."

They regrouped at the mound. Squando inspected the saddlebags of the Hessians for a clean shirt to use as bandages for both his bloody knee and Barnabas's injuries. Barnabas remembered the little jar of ointment acquired from the washhouse attendant. They both dabbed it on their wounds, and Barnabas smeared it over gashes that Little Bay and Macaroni had inflicted on one another. While they were doctoring themselves, the others collected horses, weapons, ammunition, and everything of value or not so that nothing was left to indicate that a killing had happened at the sacred mound. Although all of them respected the spirits of their ancestors and did not wish to offend them, Squando was moved by a powerful sense of connection with these unknown but not forgotten people.

The two outliers returned in triumph with the Hessian's body slung over his horse, his scalp already parted from his head. One wore the gorget around his neck. They buried the bodies behind the mound in a tangle of alders. Debris was thrown over the shallow graves to disguise the freshly turned dirt. Spybuck said a prayer in gratitude that none of his party had died except for one old horse. Those who carried tobacco sprinkled pinches of it liberally as an offering to the spirits of this place.

With these protocols accomplished, Spybuck distributed the spoils. Squando gladly received the pistol that had been long in contention between himself and Pendleton. He protested, however, at receiving Macaroni. He knew the horse's vices. Spybuck pointed out patiently that the bright chestnut was easily recognizable in these parts as the property of a British officer, now missing. The sooner the horse was out of the Ohio Country, the better for all of them. Reluctantly, Squando agreed, swapping the British tack for that stripped from the body of the old gray. The British tack was buried with the bodies. He adamantly refused the offer of one of the Jaeger rifles. He was a bowman and had already retrieved the two arrows from the body of the Hessian he had killed.

Barnabas was openly pleased to receive one of the finely crafted German rifles. He had long admired them as equal to or better than any Pennsylvania long rifle. He stroked the silky walnut stock and tested the strong spring of the frizzen. Mostly, he appreciated its greater accuracy than the smooth-bore muskets requisitioned by the army. He believed the Jaeger would do him good service in his travels westward. Even the youth Red Hand was pleased with his allotted share.

As Barnabas and Squando readied themselves for departure, Spybuck wished them well on their long, overland journey to the Mississippi. He generously offered his name as a surety should their presence be challenged. He was widely known throughout the Ohio Country as a warrior, scout, and diplomat, as well as a personal friend of the notorious Simon Girty.

The party of Wyandots was eager to return to Upper Sandusky. They would boast of their exploits in stealing horses worth many muskets and much powder. Not one word would be spoken about a missing British officer and his horse.

TWELVE

CAHOKIA

Squando and Barnabas rode into the bustling town of Cahokia on a fine fall day. The leaves were starting to put on their colors. Five hundred or more long, increasingly weary miles stretched behind them from Detroit to this old town on the eastern bank of the Mississippi. Founded by French missionaries, Cahokia was now in the control of the Americans.

Young and resilient, the two friends had healed from their injuries, resting when welcomed at Indian villages, although they had little to offer in return. Twice, they had given Spybuck's name as a password for safe passage. People opened up to Squando, whose reputation as a prophet preceded him. Circulating in that unfathomable way that news spreads by word of mouth through a sparsely populated wilderness, Squando heard disquieting rumors about Simon Girty.

"The news of your friend is not good, Barny," Squando informed him. "Some say he is dead, others that he is barely alive, others that he will never be in his right mind again. They say he was struck down from behind by the Mohawk Captain Joseph Brant," and after the briefest of pauses, "with a sword." He forbore to point out that Girty had been struck down just as his vision had foretold.

This matter occupied their talk for many miles, and Barnabas hoped for confirmation that Simon Girty still lived when they reached Cahokia, where trade brought all news.

Riding through the town, they passed numerous trading establishments, liveries, and small businesses, many identified with trade signs written in French. They paused to admire the handsome, new courthouse erected by George Rogers Clark, the American war hero who seized Cahokia from the British. They looked askance at the brothels, obviously open for business even in mid-day. Squando was uneasy that they, too, were being examined. Why would an Indian be riding such a finely bred horse?

"This horse is like a sign hung around my neck. Barny, you can bargain a better price for him than I can. Sell him and find a good Indian horse for me." Squando had never taken to the horse he had twice stolen.

Barnabas knew his friend was set upon living during the winter months with his people, Abenaki who had found safety and support among other Indians. Squando had heard that such a village was near Cahokia and that one elder there taught the hand-talk language of the Plains Indians. He was eager to learn this language for himself before crossing the great river.

When they reached the banks of the mighty Mississippi, they dismounted and stood gazing as vessels—barges, keelboats, canoes, rafts—were loaded and unloaded in the noon sun. "I have seen this place in dreams, Barny, but crowded and uglier. A screaming monster that I cannot name comes in a cloud of gray smoke down this river." He shrugged. "The future is coming fast. I would be gone from here before it arrives."

Across the river rose desultory smoke from St. Louis, the gateway westward, recently a French city now in Spanish control. Most of this trade was bound for New Orleans in the Louisiana Territory. Rivermen were in demand, but neither young man was interested in the heavy labor of the keelboat trade.

"I know scouting and trading and military life, but I've never worked a job as such," Barnabas said, "and I don't believe I'm cut out for that sort of drudgery. I've got no taste for farming. I like land that man has not shaped to suit himself. But, I'm young and able-bodied and likely to find work to get me by." He rubbed at his left ear, still sore.

"When you sell Macaroni, Barny, there should be money enough to stake you for a time here in Cahokia. It looks like a town where you will need ready cash. You speak good enough French to make yourself welcome here."

They retreated from the busy bank to the shade of trees, where they stripped the tack and Squando's gear from Macaroni. The horse pawed uneasily as Barnabas mounted him barebacked with only a rope halter to guide him. He sensed a parting to come. "I'll be back with the best horse I can find. There was a sign back there that said, 'Horses and Mules for Buy, Barter and Trade.' I'll start there."

He found a surly liveryman under the sign, impatient for his midday round at the tavern and not a sound-looking horse in the corral. A plain brown gelding alone in a pen did catch his eye. The liveryman noted the direction of Barnabas's gaze. Barnabas could see the man calculating the odds. "Now that's a fine piece of horseflesh. Not pretty, I grant you, not like this high-stepping horse who must eat his weight in oats. This horse is new come to me, and I can't guarantee him, but . . ." Barnabas cut off his spiel and asked to inspect the horse. With a sale likely, the dealer was glad to oblige.

Barnabas first felt the horse's legs and found them sound; he looked at his teeth and found them young enough; he picked up his unshod feet and found them clean; he looked into the horse's eyes and found them bright. The horse cooperated. He had not been misused and was unafraid. Barnabas walked slowly around him, assessing the slope of his shoulder, the short back, the fullness of the rump, and the angle of his hocks. He rode the plain horse up and down the street bareback at a walk, a trot, and a canter and found the horse willing and responsive. He liked the horse. He traded Macaroni without a pang of regret in exchange for this plain brown gelding and a little stack of silver coins, ignoring the liveryman who insisted he was being extorted.

When Barnabas returned with the plain horse, the gelding nickered a friendly greeting to Little Bay. Squando rose to his feet and repeated all that Barnabas had just done at the livery. He, too, liked the horse. The unnamed gelding stood patiently as they put the bridle of the old gray horse on his head and the saddle on his back and tied Squando's bed roll and bow to the saddle.

"It's a hard thing to say goodbye, even for a time, Squando," Barnabas said as he shook his friend's hand heartily. "I know where to find you and will send word of my lodgings." The two parted, Squando on his plain brown horse, eager to winter among his people, and Barnabas on Little Bay, riding back into the town of Cahokia.

TO BE CONTINUED

About the Author

MATTHEW BLAINE enjoys swapping stories with interesting people with their own stories to tell, especially around campfires. Although his education was hampered by dyslexia, he got another sort of education in the company of Ernest Hemingway, Jack London, Louis L'Amour, John Steinbeck and, when he could get them, men's adventure magazines. After stints as a cab driver, steelworker, factory floor assembler and carpenter, he worked for thirty years managing trade shows on the East Coast. During the pandemic, he wrote two self-printed memoirs about his travel and outdoor adventures. That triggered an ambition to write honest fiction in which he could reinvent himself in the lives of historical fictional characters. An avid primitive archer, canoeist, long-distance hiker, minimalist and unionist, Matthew travels with an eye for the obscure stories of the past.

Retired, he lives in a rural Pennsylvania county, haunting flea markets for goods to trade with fellow outdoorsmen at swaps and archery rendezvous. In a shop inside his woods, he practices the skills required for leather working, shaping and fletching primitive arrows, and marrying old axeheads with newly-fashioned handles.